The books in this series introduce young children to the four rules of number.

This book gives over one hundred basic facts of addition. The lively, colourful cartoon pictures illustrate the number bonds and mathematical symbols are used under each picture. There are hours of fun and learning for all young children who love counting and simple arithmetic.

Published by Ladybird Books Ltd Loughborough Leicestershire UK
Ladybird Books Inc Auburn Maine 04210 USA

Printed in England

PRACTISE AT HOME
Fun with
ADDITION

written by ROGER and MARY HURT
illustrated by LYNN N GRUNDY

2 + 2

Ladybird Books

Here is one elephant.

Along comes another elephant.

Now there are two elephants.

$1 + 1 = 2$

Here are
two children.

Here comes a friend.

Now there are three children.

$$2 + 1 = 3$$

There are no eggs in the box.

Mummy puts one egg in the box.

Now there is one egg in the box.

$$0 + 1 = 1$$

A man has three cats.

Another cat comes to stay.

Now there are four cats.

$$3 + 1 = 4$$

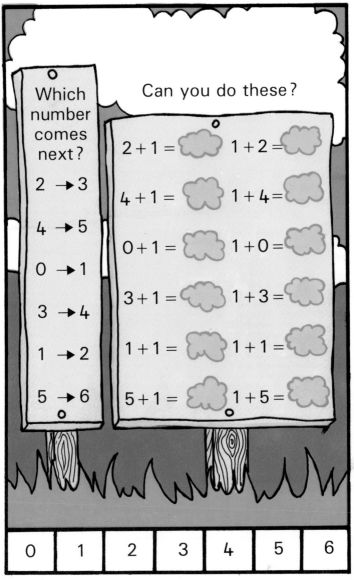

Which number comes next?

2 → 3

4 → 5

0 → 1

3 → 4

1 → 2

5 → 6

Can you do these?

2 + 1 =   1 + 2 =

4 + 1 =   1 + 4 =

0 + 1 =   1 + 0 =

3 + 1 =   1 + 3 =

1 + 1 =   1 + 1 =

5 + 1 =   1 + 5 =

| 0 | 1 | 2 | 3 | 4 | 5 | 6 |

I have two sweets in one hand

and none in the other.
I have two sweets altogether.

$$2 + 0 = 2$$

Here are two witches.

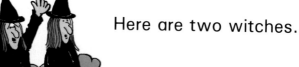

Along come
two more witches.

Now there are four witches.

$$2 + 2 = 4$$

There are no birds on the branch.

Three birds fly to the branch.

Now there are three birds.

$$0 + 3 = 3$$

There are no bottles on the step.

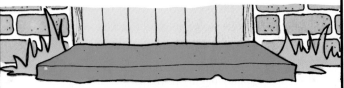

The milkman leaves two bottles.

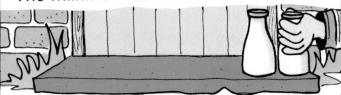

Now there are two bottles.

$$0 + 2 = 2$$

There are three blue shirts
and two red shirts on the line.

There are five shirts altogether.

$$3 + 2 = 5$$

Here are two dragons.

Along come three more.

Now there are five dragons.

$$2 + 3 = 5$$

Here are four ice-creams.

We buy one more.

Now we have five ice-creams.

$$4 + 1 = 5$$

I show five fingers on one hand
and none on the other hand.

I show five fingers altogether.

$$5 + 0 = 5$$

Which fish are caught in the nets?

A farmer has three sheep.

He buys three more sheep.

Now he has six sheep.

$$3 + 3 = 6$$

Here are four lollipops.

Daddy brings two more lollipops.

Now we have six lollipops.

$$4 + 2 = 6$$

Here are five logs.

Here is another log.

Now there are six logs.

$$5 + 1 = 6$$

There are no rabbits in the field.

Six rabbits come out of their holes.

Now there are six rabbits in the field.

$$0 + 6 = 6$$

Here are the number bonds for six.

6 + 0

3 + 3

4 + 2

5 + 1

0 + 6

2 + 4

1 + 5

Try to learn these.

One house has four windows,
the other has three windows.

There are seven windows altogether.

$$4 + 3 = 7$$

One cow has three patches.
The other cow has four patches.

There are seven patches altogether.

$$3 + 4 = 7$$

One leaf has five ladybirds.
The other has two ladybirds.

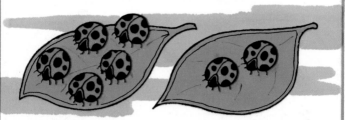

There are seven ladybirds altogether.

$$5 + 2 = 7$$

There are two dwarfs on the horse
and five dwarfs in the cart.

These are the seven dwarfs.
Do you know their names?

$$2 + 5 = 7$$

These are the number bonds for seven.

Try to learn these bonds.

Count on two.

3 → 5

4 → 6

2 → 4

6 → 8

1 → 3

8 → 10

7 → 9

5 → 7

0 → 2

Can you do these?

3 + 2 =	2 + 3 =
4 + 2 =	2 + 4 =
2 + 2 =	2 + 2 =
6 + 2 =	2 + 6 =
1 + 2 =	2 + 1 =
8 + 2 =	2 + 8 =
7 + 2 =	2 + 7 =
5 + 2 =	2 + 5 =
0 + 2 =	2 + 0 =

0	1	2	3	4	5	6	7	8	9	10

20

Here are five cups.

Here are three more cups.

There are eight cups altogether.

$$5 + 3 = 8$$

Here are seven books on a shelf.

One more book is on the table.

There are eight books altogether.

$$7 + 1 = 8$$

Here are the number bonds for eight.

8 + 0
3 + 5
7 + 1
4 + 4
6 + 2
0 + 8
1 + 7
5 + 3
2 + 6

Try to learn these.

Here are two lots of flowers.

There are nine flowers altogether.

$$3 + 6 = 9$$

Some bees are flying to the hive.

There are nine bees in the picture.

$$4 + 5 = 9$$

Which clowns are holding the balloons?

25

These are the number bonds for nine.

Try to remember them.

What are the missing numbers?

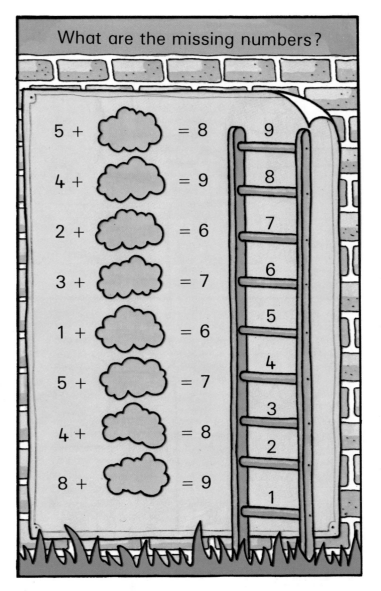

5 + ☁ = 8

4 + ☁ = 9

2 + ☁ = 6

3 + ☁ = 7

1 + ☁ = 6

5 + ☁ = 7

4 + ☁ = 8

8 + ☁ = 9

9
8
7
6
5
4
3
2
1

27

Daniel has six crayons.
Kate has four.

$6 + 4 = 10$ **or** $4 + 6 = 10$

Kate has seven crayons.
Daniel has three.

$7 + 3 = 10$ **or** $3 + 7 = 10$

Daniel has eight crayons.
Kate has two.

$8 + 2 = 10$ **or** $2 + 8 = 10$

Kate has nine crayons.
Daniel has one.

$9 + 1 = 10$ **or** $1 + 9 = 10$

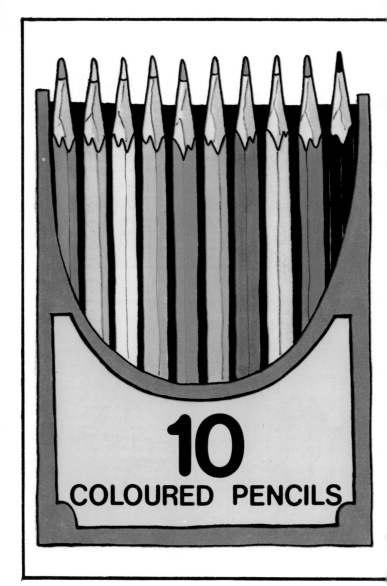

10
COLOURED PENCILS

Do you know the missing numbers?

+ 1 = 10   + 0 = 10

+ 8 = 10   + 4 = 10

+ 3 = 10   + 2 = 10

+ 6 = 10   + 7 = 10

+ 10 = 10   + 9 = 10

+ 5 = 10

Which apples fall into which baskets?

33

$$10 + 1 = 11$$

$$10 + 2 = 12$$

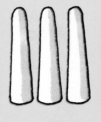

$$10 + 3 = 13$$

 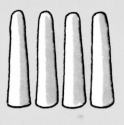

10 + 4 = 14

 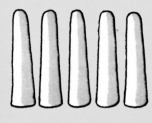

10 + 5 = 15

 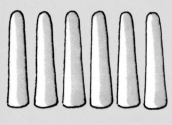

10 + 6 = 16

Here are two bunches of grapes.

There are eleven grapes altogether.

$7 + 4 = 11$ **or** $4 + 7 = 11$

Some sausages are on the plates.

There are eleven sausages on the plates.

$8 + 3 = 11$ **or** $3 + 8 = 11$

Here are some flags with stars on them.

There are twelve stars altogether on the flags.

$$9 + 3 = 12 \quad \textbf{or} \quad 3 + 9 = 12$$

Here are some eggs.

There are twelve eggs altogether.

$$6 + 6 = 12$$

Here are some apples.

There are eleven apples in the boxes.

$6 + 5 = 11$ **or** $5 + 6 = 11$

Here are some cakes.

There are eleven cakes altogether.

$9 + 2 = 11$ **or** $2 + 9 = 11$

Here are some buttons on shirts.

There are twelve buttons altogether on the shirts.

$$7 + 5 = 12 \quad \textbf{or} \quad 5 + 7 = 12$$

Here are some leaves on twigs.

There are twelve leaves on the twigs.

$$8 + 4 = 12 \quad \textbf{or} \quad 4 + 8 = 12$$

40

Who lives in the houses?

What are the missing numbers?

7 + ☁ = 12

4 + ☁ = 11

6 + ☁ = 12

8 + ☁ = 11

3 + ☁ = 12

5 + ☁ = 11

2 + ☁ = 12

7 + ☁ = 11

8 + ☁ = 12

9 + ☁ = 11

12
11
10
9
8
7
6
5
4
3
2
1

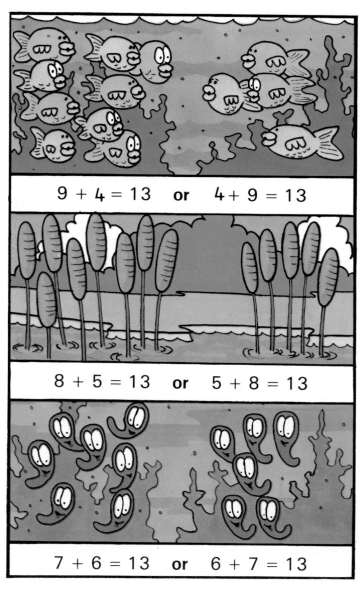

$9 + 4 = 13$ **or** $4 + 9 = 13$

$8 + 5 = 13$ **or** $5 + 8 = 13$

$7 + 6 = 13$ **or** $6 + 7 = 13$

43

9 + 5 = 14

5 + 9 = 14

8 + 6 = 14

6 + 8 = 14

7 + 7 = 14

What are the missing numbers?

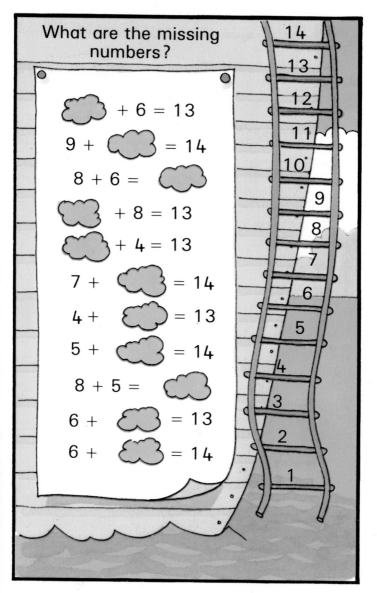

$\text{?} + 6 = 13$

$9 + \text{?} = 14$

$8 + 6 = \text{?}$

$\text{?} + 8 = 13$

$\text{?} + 4 = 13$

$7 + \text{?} = 14$

$4 + \text{?} = 13$

$5 + \text{?} = 14$

$8 + 5 = \text{?}$

$6 + \text{?} = 13$

$6 + \text{?} = 14$

45

46

47

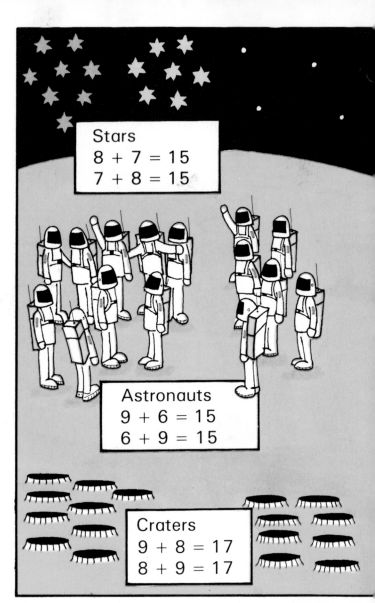

Stars
8 + 7 = 15
7 + 8 = 15

Astronauts
9 + 6 = 15
6 + 9 = 15

Craters
9 + 8 = 17
8 + 9 = 17

48

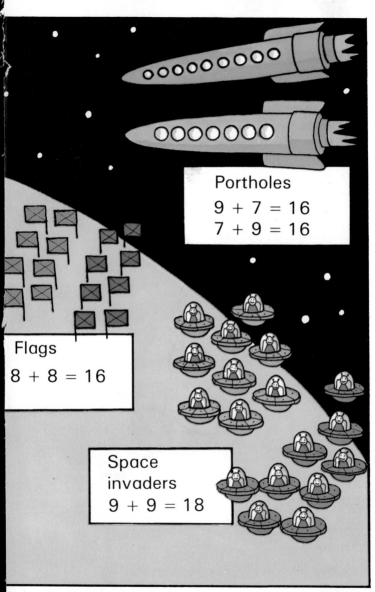

Portholes
9 + 7 = 16
7 + 9 = 16

Flags
8 + 8 = 16

Space
invaders
9 + 9 = 18

49

Which rockets go to which planets?